George Washington, Thomas Hamilton Murray

The Irish Washingtons At Home And Abroad

George Washington, Thomas Hamilton Murray

The Irish Washingtons At Home And Abroad

ISBN/EAN: 9783741187537

Manufactured in Europe, USA, Canada, Australia, Japa

Cover: Foto ©Andreas Hilbeck / pixelio.de

Manufactured and distributed by brebook publishing software
(www.brebook.com)

George Washington, Thomas Hamilton Murray

The Irish Washingtons At Home And Abroad

THE IRISH WASHINGTONS

AT HOME AND ABROAD,

TOGETHER WITH SOME MENTION OF THE

ANCESTRY OF THE AMERICAN PATER PATRIÆ.

BY

GEORGE WASHINGTON,

OF DUBLIN, IRELAND,

AND

THOMAS HAMILTON MURRAY,

BOSTON, MASS.

————◆————

BOSTON :

THE CARROLLTON PRESS,

1898.

DEDICATED

AMERICAN-IRISH HISTORICAL SOCIETY.

TRIBUTE TO THE PATER PATRIÆ.

HOW HIS DEEDS HAVE RENDERED THE WASHINGTON
NAME GLORIOUS FOR ALL TIME. — WASHINGTONS
IN IRELAND FOR TWO OR THREE CENTURIES. —
INTERESTING DATA.

BY THOMAS HAMILTON MURRAY.

The name Washington is dear to the heart of every
patriotic American. While the republic endures, this will
never be otherwise. The life and works of the *Pater
Patriæ* are secure in the temple of liberty. His name and
fame serve as beacon lights for the oppressed in every
land, and illumine the path to freedom.

It is a fact not generally known that Washington, as a
family name, has long existed in Ireland. It is mentioned
in the records of many counties, and bearers of the name
are still frequently met. These Irish Washingtons have
produced many people of ability, and in creed are nearly
all Roman Catholics.

The first Washingtons in Ireland are believed to have
gone there from England between two hundred and fifty
and three hundred years ago, perhaps earlier. Their
descendants became thoroughly Irish and have been allied
in marriage with the Fords, Cronins, Kellys, Hogans,
MacCormacks, MacNamaras, Mahons, Sullivans, Fitz-
geralds, and other historic Irish families. The Irish
Washingtons, too, have been identified with leading movements in behalf of Irish freedom. One of them was connected with the patriotic Fenian organization, while the

name has also figured in the work of the Land League and in that of its successor, the Irish National League.

Knowing the interest this whole topic would have for the American people, I resolved some time ago to collect as much material as possible bearing on the subject, and to present the result in the present modest form. I am indebted for assistance in my researches to the Most Rev. John Clancy, D. D., bishop of the Irish diocese of Elphin ; to the Rev. John Maher, P. P., of Kilglass and Russky, in Bishop Clancy's diocese, and to Mr. John O'Hart, the eminent Irish genealogist of Clontarf, Ireland.

Mr. O'Hart referred me to Mr. George Washington, of Dublin, from whom I obtained many facts of great interest and importance. Mr. George W. Washington, of Melbourne, Australia, has also given me much data, and I am likewise indebted for interesting facts to Miss Julia M. MacNamara, now of Manchester, N. H. Miss MacNamara, it should be stated, is a daughter of Nicholas J. and Margaret (Washington) MacNamara. For facts regarding Irish Washingtons who settled in the United States, I am under obligations to Washingtons now residing in Providence, R. I., and elsewhere.

The accompanying chapter by Mr. George Washington, of Dublin, is a mine of information. Mr. Washington is a gentleman of quiet and scholarly tastes, and is naturally averse to publicity. However, at my earnest request, seconded by that of my friend, Mr. O'Hart, he was finally prevailed upon to overcome his reluctance, and to furnish the accompanying extremely interesting sketch. He was induced to do this, chiefly, upon the bona fide representation that whatever he wrote on the subject would prove of great interest to the people of the United States. That it is certain to so prove, no American will dispute.

In the Evening *Herald*, one of the leading papers of the

Irish capital, a communication appeared May 31, 1892, headed "The Romance of History." It was signed "Sulgrave," and the following is gleaned therefrom : —

* * * * * * * *

"Few, reading your most interesting account in Saturday's issue of the finding and publishing of the Verney letters, know what an influence that young gentleman, who mourned so pathetically the death of his wife, exercised, indirectly, in altering and shaping the destinies of the world for all future time. Certainly he had no idea of it himself.

"Had he been sent to Cambridge University instead of to Oxford ; had he been a roysterer instead of the sweet, engaging young man that he was ; had anything about him been different, he never would have brought frequently with him to his house at Middle Claydon the Rev. Lawrence Washington, M. A., who never would have seen there the bailiff's pretty daughter, and never married her ; and never would their children have been driven away, boycotted and poor, from the shores where their relatives held rank, wealth, and influence, to seek a home in the Western world, which was one day to owe so much to their illustrious descendant.

"How that harsh treatment entered the souls of the emigrants is indicated by the fact that they never told their children from what family or from what part of England they came. The subject was tabooed or referred to unwillingly, so that even General Washington, who was born within seventy-five years of their landing in America, died in the vague belief that his ancestors came from Yorkshire, Lancashire or some still more northerly county.

"'In the beginning of 1655,' says Moncure D. Conway, 'John Washington [the emigrant] found himself with £28 left him by his stepfather, and his share of what his mother

Amphillis had saved from the £60 left her, and the fifth of her Purleigh tithes received during the four preceding years.' For the next four years nothing whatever is known of his movements ; but it is certain from his will that he married, and brought his wife, two children, and his surviving sister, Martha, to Virginia with him in 1659. ' But,' says Conway, ' he might not have come had not certain fine Sir and Lady Washingtons turned up their noses at the impecunious son of a bailiff's daughter.'

"Sir Edmund Verney . . . was standard bearer to Charles I. I saw a portrait of him about two months ago, as he appeared before Edge Hill, where he was doomed to fall (1642). His third son, Sir Edmund, commanded a troop of horse at Drogheda, where he fell beneath the swords of Cromwell's Ironsides. The family had large estates in Breffni at this time, and not long after one of them was raised to the peerage as Baron Belturbet and Viscount Fermanagh. The writer is acquainted with one family of Washingtons, which was resident in this district one hundred and fifty years ago, amongst whom it has always been a tradition that their ancestor came from Brington in Northamptonshire.

"Sir William Washington had two sons and a daughter, Elizabeth, who married Major William Legge [an Irishman]. Henry, the elder, became a colonel, and was much distinguished during the civil war. In conjunction with Colonel Mark Trevor and Colonel Francis Trafford, ' a professed Papist,' he is found in Denbighshire, where he had influence, raising a force for the king, which was afterwards utilized at Marston Moor, where Mark Trevor covered himself with glory by wounding Oliver Cromwell, for which, at the Restoration, he was made Baron Rostrevor, in the County Down [Ireland], and Viscount Dungannon. Near the latter place [in Ireland], I am informed, is the

hamlet of Washington, possibly called after his old companion-in-arms, and a family of the name is, to this day, living within a few miles of Rostrevor.

"Walter and George Washington, of Warwick, England, lost their lives and property in the Royal cause, and I have reason to believe that their descendants are to be found at present in a remote part of Galway, Ireland. There are Washington families in Roscommon, and your readers may be interested to know that the writer became aware of their existence through their names appearing in the deputation from their district to meet Mr. Parnell in Strokestown during his final campaign. I am informed that they claim to have migrated John Washington, the ancestor of the President, to America, and it has been claimed for them by at least one writer in the United States. It may not be so preposterous after all, as for four years before emigrating no trace whatever can be found of John in England, so that the general may have been half Irish by descent, which would, indeed, be curious."

[There is also a theory, but with how much basis of fact has not yet been determined, that this John Washington left England and resided in Ireland, perhaps with relatives; that he married in Ireland, and that he may have had children born there.]

"Of the Yorkshire family, from which the President thought himself descended, I have collected many interesting remains. Though there is no established connection between them and Northampton, their crests and seals are very similar, and their similarity in suffering for the Royal cause is beyond question. Of the two families I believe Yorkshire has suffered most. In fact the civil war practically rooted out that family in England, and those left never recovered their stations. There is not at present one Washington left in Northamptonshire, nor one county

family of the name, and in the new Doomsday Book, published in 1875, the name only appears, I think, fifteen times. Those of the Washingtons who immigrated to Ireland easily fell in with the people, and the Reformation having been so recent it is not surprising that in a different atmosphere from England they speedily embraced the old faith."

*   *   *   *   *   *   *   *

"Sulgrave" expresses his belief that some of the Galway Washingtons are descended from Walter and George Washington, of Warwick. It is a curious fact that some of the Irish Washingtons now in the State of Rhode Island are of Galway blood. Mr. Michael Washington, for instance, came from County Galway fifty or sixty years ago and located in Providence, R. I., where many of his descendants still reside. In the old country he had wedded Catherine Ford. Their children were Edward, Bridget, Julia, Patrick, and Michael.

I find there are two villages in Ireland called Washington. One of these is in the County Tyrone, near Dungannon, and the other in the County Kildare. Good evidence this of the prominence of the name at one time in Irish affairs. During my researches in the United States, I have found Irish Washingtons or their descendants in Bangor, Me.; Manchester, N. H.; Fall River, Mass.; Newport, Providence, and Pawtucket, R. I.; St. Paul, Minn.; Nashville, Tenn.; McKeesport, Pa., and in the States of New York, Colorado, and Montana.

A pathetic occurrence in the history of the Irish Washingtons in the Old Land was the death of little Anne Washington caused by British soldiers in the Rebellion of 1798. The child was but seven or eight years of age, and was stopping with her grandparents in the County Wicklow. One day the house was surrounded by a British

force, with the result that the little girl was shot and killed. Many other notable incidents might be narrated, but they can better be told by Mr. George Washington, whose valued contribution here follows.

BOSTON, MASS., Oct. 19, 1898.

Anniversary of the surrender of LORD CORNWALLIS
to GEN. GEORGE WASHINGTON at Yorktown.

HENRY WILLIAM WASHINGTON,
Sometimes called " The General."
Born in Cavan, Ireland.   Deceased.

SOME IRISH WASHINGTONS.

AN ENTERTAINING MONOGRAPH ON THEIR DERIVATION
AND CAREER. — REFERENCE TO THE AMERICAN
PRESIDENT AND HIS ANCESTRY. — EXTRACTS
FROM THE RECORDS.

BY GEORGE WASHINGTON.

The widespread interest taken by the American public
in everything pertaining to the name of Washington must
be, mainly, my justification for this article. I have, also,
a hope that its publication may lead to further light being
thrown on the circumstances of the settlement of the
Washingtons in Ireland, and a desire to place on record,
in some permanent form, the few facts I have been able to
gather regarding the Irish Washingtons, so that those who
come after us may know a little of the people from whom
they are descended.

The family takes its name from the village of Washington, in the County Durham, England. In the year 1166,
according to the *Bolden Buke*, William de Hertburn, the
founder of the family, exchanged his village and manor of
Hertburn on the river Tees for the village and manor of
Wessyngton. He thenceforward assumed the name of
de Wessyngton, and for two hundred years his descendants
who held their lands in knights' fee from the Bishop of
Durham, sat in the councils of the palatinate.

By 1400 this family was extinct in the male line, but in
the neighboring counties of Westmoreland and Lancaster
two branches had sprung up whose descendants are trace-

able to the present day. In 1300 the Westmoreland branch were lords of Milburne, and Walter de Wessyngton held the lands of Helton and Fletham. For two hundred years afterwards the chief seat of the family appears to have been at Hallad Hall, Westmoreland.

Towards the middle of the sixteenth century Richard Washington, of Hallad Hall, settled at Adwick le Street, in Yorkshire, and founded the Yorkshire branch. His grandsons, William and Richard, came to Ireland and founded a branch here. His great grandson Robert, " a merchant in Holland," emigrated to the Continent and founded the family of Count von Washington, of Munich. The race flourished in Yorkshire as late as the middle of the last century, perhaps later.

The Lancashire branch was descended from Robert de Wessyngton, Lord of Milburne, who had lands in Kerneford (Carnforth), County Lancaster, in right of his wife Amicia, daughter of Hugh, Lord de Kerneford. He had a son Robert, who had a son John of Warton in Lonsdale, living 1386, who had a son John, living 1403, who had a son John, wounded at Agincourt, Oct. 25, 1415, who had Robert of Tuwhitfield, who died 1483, who had Robert of Tuwhitfield, who had

John of Tuwhitfield, son and heir, who married Margaret, daughter of Robert Kitson, of Warton, and sister of Sir Thomas Kitson, of Hengrave Hall, Suffolk, Alderman of the city of London, — Sheriff, 1533, — commonly called " Kitson the Merchant." John Washington went to London and became a prosperous wool merchant. He had

Lawrence of Gray's Inn, Mayor of Northampton, 1532 and 1545. Had a grant of the manor of Sulgrave, County Northampton, 1539, and died July 19, 1584. His second son, Sir Lawrence, of Wedbury, Bucks, and Garsden, Wilts. entered Gray's Inn, 1571 ; called to the bar, 1582 ; ap-

pointed Registrar to the Court of Chancery, 1593 ; M. P. for Maidstone, 1603; d. 1619; founded the family of Washington of Garsden, Wilts. The Mayor's eldest son was

Robert of Sulgrave, who, in conjunction with his eldest son, Lawrence, sold Sulgrave in 1610 to his nephew, Lawrence Makepeace. His second son, Walter, founded the Warwickshire family. Lawrence, the eldest son of Robert, now moved to Brington in 1610. He had seventeen children. His fifth son, Lawrence, of Brasenose College, Oxford, rector of Purleigh, 1633–1643, was father of John, the emigrant to Virginia, who was great grand-father of General Washington.

The last of the Warton family, a clergyman, died about the middle of the present century. The Kent family are of Lancashire stock.

* * * * * * * *

Until quite recently I was under the impression that my own immediate family was the only Washington one in Ireland, but my attention was called to the fact that three men of the name were on the platform with Mr. Parnell at his last meeting in Strokestown, County Roscommon.

Through a friend I afterwards got a list of the births and deaths of Washingtons in Ireland for many years past, thus locating the different branches. Practically there are only five : one at Bryansford, County Down : a second in Kilglass parish, County Roscommon ; a third at New Ross, County Wexford ; another near Carlow, and my own in Dublin. There was another at Kilbeacanty, near Gort, County Galway, but a correspondent informs me they have left there and probably emigrated. No one family, I believe, knew of the other's existence, and each thought it was the only bearer of the name in the country. They are all Roman Catholics and mostly farmers.

The Bryansford family can only trace back about seventy years, and are probably an offshoot from some of the other branches. The present tenant's grandmother, a widow, settled in that place with her two very young children, a boy and a girl, about the year 1830. They had previously lived in Dundalk, County Louth, a town principally on the estate of the Earl of Roden. The names in use amongst them are James, Joseph, Sarah.

The Western Irish branch has a longer record, and dozens of this family are at present in England and the United States, so that what I have to say must be deeply interesting to them. Mr. Dudley Washington, of Kilgarrow, Kilglass, County Roscommon, writes that he is seventy years old and remembers his grandfather, who was over eighty years when he himself was young. His people, he believed, had lived in the neighborhood for three hundred years past, having come there, he had heard, after some great disturbance in England. His ancestors had been Protestants.

I had frequently seen in Mr. O'Hart's *Irish Pedigrees*, that a Capt. Henry Washington was amongst the Royalist officers serving in Ireland between 1641–9, called the "'49 officers"; and knowing that at the Restoration all arrears of pay were settled by grants of forfeited lands, I determined to see where his grant lay, and through the kindness of the Deputy Keeper of the Records of Ireland, J. J. Digges Latouche, Esq., A.M., LL.D., who generously allowed me to examine all documents, I located him.

He was in the thirty-third batch of officers dealt with. His claim was for £374, 9s. 2d., and he appears in conjunction with John Griffith, £463, 9s., and Lieut. Daniel Moore, £104, 10s., to have disposed of his interest to a Sir Martin Noell, of Chancery Lane, London, almost next door to Laurence Washington, the Chancery Registrar.

GEORGE THOMAS WASHINGTON,
Son of Henry William Washington, "The General,"
Born Feb. 11, 1847.

The collective grant consisted of lands in the barony of Moydow, County Longford, including the townlands of Ballintober, Tonemeranagh, Cartron, Koole, Keyley, Shanaghmore, Ballyboyy, Loughseiden, Carrick Edmond, Lislea, Loughuagh, etc., in all 2767 a. 1 r. 24 per., at the yearly rent of £34, 11s. 10¼d., together with £1,000 out of the houses and lands sold, or about to be sold, in the city of Limerick, said sums to be paid by Wentworth, Earl of Roscommon, a nephew of the Earl of Strafford, and Roger, Earl of Ossory. Grant dated 18 Chas. II. (1667).

Wentworth, Earl of Roscommon, was the son of James Dillon, the intimate friend of the Verneys of Middle Claydon. James must have well known the rector of Purleigh, General Washington's ancestor, who visited at Claydon, since he courted the rector's cousin Doll Leake, who lived there, and gave great offence to the Verneys by jilting her and marrying Sir Thomas Wentworth's sister.

Now a strange thing about the grant is, that some of these lands, though in Longford, are in the parish of Kilglass, and it is in the parish of Kilglass, barony of Ballintober, County Roscommon, just across the border, these Washingtons have resided for more than two centuries. The Christian names in use amongst them are : George, Francis, James, William, Edward, Thomas, Michael, John, Patrick, Catherine, Elizabeth, Bridget, Mary, Anne, Jane, Emilia.

I next found a charter signed by King Charles I. and Sir Thomas Wentworth, granting to William Washington the office of customer or chief tax collector of the port of Limerick. It is dated 1636, the same year, I see, that the first Washington turned up in Virginia, and I believe a member of the same family.

This William, who thus came to Ireland under the patronage of Sir Thomas Wentworth, the Lord Deputy,

was no doubt from Yorkshire, for on turning to the Visitation of York, 1666 (Dugdale), I find a William of that time described as having lived in Ireland and left descendants there, and I suppose some of the Irish Washingtons owe their origin to him. His eldest brother, Darcy, had married Anne, daughter of Matthew Wentworth, of Bretton, a relative of the Lord Deputy, and I have no doubt it was this connection that brought him to Ireland.

In the year 1640 a Richard Washington, B. D., turns up in Dublin as provost of Trinity College, and as the office was practically in the gift of the Lord Deputy, now created Earl of Strafford, I think we may fairly conclude that he was William's younger brother, who in the pedigree is described as having died unmarried. He left the college in the following year (1641) and returned to Oxford, having fallen, no doubt, with Strafford's party.

* * * * * * * *

Moncure D. Conway, in an article in Harper's for May, 1891, mentions a Richard Washington, of University College Oxford (1646), as " the only one of the old stock left." He says, " I have not placed this Royalist, apparently a clergyman. He died, 1651, and was buried at St. Dunstan's in the West, London." A recently published history of Trinity College identifies this man with the provost, the date and place of death being exactly the same in both cases.

As some corroboration of his supposed Yorkshire origin, I quote the following from the *Miscellanea Genealogica* : "Will of John Hovendon of University College, Oxford, dated Dec. 26, 1629. Proved by Thos. Radcliffe." He appoints "my friend Thomas Radcliffe sole executor. My friend, Dr. Bancroft, master of University College, and Mr. Richard Washington, overseers," and "gives rings to Mr. Richard Washington and Mr. Philip Wentworth." The

Wentworths and Radcliffes were closely connected, and Sir George Radcliffe, the Earl of Strafford's secretary, has been described as his "right hand." This conjunction of names should go far, I think, to support my contention as to his identity, especially as it fits in exactly with the recorded pedigree.

I will here state my belief that it would have been impossible for this gentleman not to have known the rector of Purleigh, General Washington's ancestor. They were, no doubt, friends, and could probably trace the relationship existing between them, the separation of the branches not having been so very remote. They must have had many friends in common, and I cannot but think that when visiting their relatives at Oxford, other members of both families must have become acquainted. Thus the two great branches of the family were personally known to one another at that time. Now, the Earl of Strafford's aunt (his mother's sister) was Lady Jocelyn, whose lineal descendant to-day is the Earl of Roden, on whose estate, in the County Down, Ireland, Mr. Washington, of Bryansford, is a tenant.

In 1636, while William Washington was "Customer" of Limerick, George Staunton was "Searcher" of Galway. He was of a Warwickshire family, who had formed connections by marriage with the Washingtons of the same county. His descendants have continued to live in the county of Galway, and one of them became the famous ambassador to China. Towards the middle of the last century, a Miss Catherine Staunton, of the Stauntons who were connected with the Warwickshire Washingtons, an heiress, married a Mr. Lambert and brought him an estate, and, strange to say, it was a Mr. Lambert, a descendant of this man, who, till lately, was the landlord of the Gort family of Irish Washingtons, recently emigrated. Whether these are merely coincidences I cannot say.

I next came on the will of Laurence Washington, of Garsden, Wilts (1667), and a bond for £500 lent by him to Henry Moore, a relative, whose descendant to-day is known as the Marquis of Drogheda, secured by valuable rents and tolls in the County Westmeath, which was subsequently redeemed. The daughter of this Laurence married Robert Shirley, who had large estates in the County Monaghan, and her son, Washington Shirley, sat in the Irish Parliament, dissolved in 1714, and eventually became Earl Ferrers. The Legges, the Villiers, the Spencers, the Verneys and other relatives held vast estates here. Thus the Northampton Washingtons had a direct and substantial connection with Ireland.

My next find was the will of James Washington, Gent., of the city of Kilkenny, a wealthy man, who had a brother Richard and a nephew James. He evidently had no son, but daughters, Mary and Anne, unmarried ; Sarah (Hamilton), a widow, and Margaret, wife of John Lightburne, of the town of Wexford, merchant ; and a sister, Catherine Grace.

Besides houses and lands in and around the city of Kilkenny he had "a house and premises in the town of Wexford, held on lease for a long term of years." I am inclined to think that the New Ross, County Wexford, Irish Washingtons, and one or two individuals still living in the County Kilkenny, are descended from this Richard, but of course this is conjecture. Will dated Nov. 20, 1760, proved 1761. A comparison of these Christian names with William of Limerick's nephews and nieces, one hundred years before, would certainly suggest a Yorkshire origin for this family. Their names were James, Robert, Darcy, Anne, Grace, Mary, and Sarah.

* * * * * * * *

Of my own family I can speak more precisely. My great-grandfather was born in Northamptonshire in or

about the year 1743. He came to Ireland from Wales about 1770. He always maintained that he was a relative of General Washington, and that the latter's ancestors, like his own, were of the Northampton stock. They both came he said, of a family who once lived on Earl Spencer's estate, and I have always heard this story without variation from the oldest members of the family I have ever met. One, I am sure, who never got her information from reading, even mentioned the place Brington to me, years before I ever heard a word about General Washington's English origin.

Not one of these old people, I suppose, ever heard of the controversy about the general's extraction, but merely handed down the facts as a matter of tradition. There is a good deal of internal evidence in the family history, which I am sifting, to support their statements. And I am not without a hope that a mention of the family may be found amongst the genealogical papers of a late distinguished scholar. I am also informed by one who knew him that my grand-uncle Henry so closely resembled the published portraits of General Washington, the American, that he was called "The General," and that his features were a good counterpart of General Washington's, as they appear on the American postage stamps of to-day. My aunt MacNamara, lately deceased, also bore the same extraordinary resemblance.

My own pedigree, so far as it is connected with Ireland, is as follows : My great-grandfather,

I. THOMAS GEORGE Washington, was born in Northamptonshire, 1743; died, 1838, aged ninety-five years : buried at Glasnevin, Dublin; married, 1789, Honoria Monks, of Wicklow, who was buried with him in 1848, aged seventy-eight. They had nine children, viz. :

  1. Thomas, of whom hereafter.

2. Henry, who settled in London; had issue: 1, Henry (married), who went to Australia: 2, George (married), now in London.
3. Michael.
4. George, who left George, Alice, and Henry.

1. Mary Martha, who married James Ford, of Newtown Butler, County Fermanagh (later of Dublin).
2. Margaret, died young.
3. Catherine, died young.
4. Bridget, married Patrick McCormack; no issue.
5. Anne, killed by yeomen in the Rebellion of 1798.

Mary Martha Washington, mentioned above, who married James Ford, of Fermanagh, became the mother of,

1. Thomas George, who went to the United States in 1850 and wedded Rosalie Redwood Anderson, of Newport, R. I. Her great grand-uncle, William Ellery, was one of the signers of the Declaration of Independence. A great-great-grandfather of hers, Baron von Weissenfels, of the Prussian army, served in the army of the Revolution, and was at one time a member of General Washington's staff.
2. James, died at sea.
3. John, died unmarried.
4. Henry, married Louisa Cronin, no issue.

1. Ellen, wife of John Kelly; had issue: (1) James; (2) Ellen, wife of Henry Prossor, who has a daughter Norah.
2. Mary, wife of Michael J. Hogan, died 1897; had issue: (1) Henry; (2) George; (3) James; (4) Mary E. The latter died in Paris, 1897.

Thomas George Washington, the founder of the family, was succeeded by his eldest son:

II. Thomas, who married, 1821, Maria Cooke, and died in 1852; had issue:
1. Thomas, who died 1839, aged eighteen years.
2. George, professor of music under the Board of National Education, Ireland, died at Belfast, 1871, unmarried.
3. James, of whom hereafter.

4. Mary, a daughter of Thomas and Maria (Cooke) Washington, married, in New York, Anthony McAlister, and had issue :

    1. Mary Ellen, wife of Frank Hollywood, ex-Member of Congress from Montana, U. S.A., now of Victor, Col. No issue living.

    2. Anthony, commander steamship Naderi, Bombay and Persian Steam Navigation Company, married, 1891, Lizzie Colclough, of Belfast, Ireland, and has issue (two daughters), Ellen and Lizzie, and a son, George Washington.

5. Margaret Washington, a daughter of Thomas and Maria (Cooke) Washington, married Nicholas J. MacNamara, solicitor of Galway. She died in 1891. They had issue :

    1. Andrew Washington MacNamara, now in New York.

    2. George Washington MacNamara, died, 1883.

    1. Julia M., now in Manchester, N. H.

    2. Cecilia Marie, in St. Paul, Minn.

    3. Margaret.

    4. Angelina, wife of George Leonard has two daughters, Constance and Aileen.

    5. Evelyn.

    6. Adelaide E.

    7. Clarinda M.

6. Jane Washington, sister of Margaret (Washington) MacNamara, is the wife of a Mr. Connor, of Nashville, Tenn. The children are Roderick, Joseph, William, Mary and George.

Thomas Washington, who succeeded his father, Thomas George Washington, the founder, as head of the Dublin family, was in turn succeeded by his third son, James.

III. This James Washington was a professor of music under the Board of National Education, Ireland ; born, 1831; died at Waterford, 1877 ; married, 1853, at Rathmines, Roman Catholic Church, to Ellen Mahon (who died, 1887). She was a daughter of James Mahon, of " Dycer's," Stephen's Green, Dublin (formerly of Kings County), and his wife, Mary Mahony, and sister of the late John C. Mahon, M. A., C. E., T. C. D., inspector under the Irish Board of Works. James Washington had issue :

24

1. George, died young.
2. James, of whom hereafter.
3. George, living 1898, unmarried, (the writer of this sketch).
4. Albert, died young.
5. Thomas, died 1895.
6. John Joseph, died young.

1. Mary, died young.
2. Mary Ellen, living 1897.
3. Margaret, died unmarried, 1883.
4. Jane, living 1897.

James (III) was succeeded by his eldest surviving son:

IV. James (2), who was born in Dublin, 1859; married, 1891, Ellen
Fitzgerald, of Drumcannon House, Tramore, County Water-
ford. He died 8th September, 1893, and left issue, a son
James George Washington, born 30th August, 1893.

I have recently come across an entry in the *Hibernian
Magazine*, which records a marriage between William
Hobbs, of the city of Waterford, and Anne Washington, of
Kilkenny, September, 1779. I also found the will of
Sarah (Washington) Hamilton, of Kilkenny, widow, her
sister, in which she leaves to her nephew, Stafford Lightburne, house, messuage, and tenements in the town of Wexford; to her brother-in-law, William Hobbs, of Waterford
and Ballyharty, County Wexford, all her estate in the
lands of Danningstown, Brickhays, part of Keatingstown,
etc., etc., held on long lease from the Earl of Courtown.

She mentions her sister, Mary Ward, otherwise Washington, wife of Alexander Ward, Esq., nephew James
Washington, son of Uncle Richard Washington, deceased,
and niece Frances Ward. (William Hobbs and Anne
Hobbs, executors, Dec. 10, 1761.) Mr. Griffith, clerk of
the Thomastown (County Kilkenny) Union, informs me
that he has always known of a Washington family living
in that district, and that a Washington was hanged as a
rebel on the bridge of New Ross, in historic 1798.

JAMES GEORGE WASHINGTON.
Born Aug. 30, 1893.
Son of James and Ellen (Fitzgerald) Washington, and nephew of
George Washington, writer of the enclosed sketch.

A branch of the Irish Washingtons, relatives of ours, is now located at Manchester, England. The founder of it was George Washington, son of Thomas George and Honoria (Monks) Washington. The pedigree of this Manchester branch is as follows : —

I. George Washington, married Alice Doxey. Their children were
  1. George, who wedded Mary Raby.
  2. Alice, married Wm. Baguley.
  3. Henry, deceased.

II. George, who wedded Mary Raby, had
  1. Gertrude.
  2. Ethel.
  .3. Alice.
  4. George. deceased.
  5. Harry.
  6. Martha. deceased.
  7. Mary, deceased.

Alice, sister of George, who married Wm. Baguley, has issue :
  1. William.
  2. Richard.
  3. Alice.
  4. Lily.
  5. Amy.
  6. Mabel.
  7. Ruth.

Of these Manchester Washingtons, George (II.) is an educator. He attended college in London, and upon leaving took charge of his present school where he has remained twenty-three years. He also has charge of the Technical School at Ramsbottom, Manchester, England, and of a pupil teachers' centre class in a neighboring place.

This practically exhausts all I have to say about the Irish Washingtons and I shall be very pleased if its publication elicits any new facts concerning them.

DALKEY, COUNTY DUBLIN, IRELAND, SEPT. 15, 1898.

To Mr. T. H. MURRAY,
  SECRETARY, AMERICAN-IRISH HISTORICAL SOCIETY, BOSTON, MASS.

FURTHER INTERESTING DETAILS.

LETTERS FROM VARIOUS BEARERS OF THE NAME — FACTS
CONCERNING DESCENDANTS OF THE IRISH WASHINGTONS
IN THE UNITED STATES AND AUSTRALIA.

BY THOMAS HAMILTON MURRAY.

In connection with this subject of the Irish Washingtons, I have in my possession several interesting letters from Mr. George W. Washington of Melbourne, Australia; Mr. Joseph Washington, of Bryansford, Ireland, and Mr. Dudley Washington, of Kilglass parish, County Roscommon.

*   *   *   *   *   *   *   *

The Melbourne George is a cousin of George of Dublin, author of the foregoing chapter. In his letter dated " The Rest, Vine St., Moonee Ponds, Melbourne," the Australian gentleman informs me that his grandfather, Henry William Washington, son of Thomas George and Honoria (Monks) Washington, was born in County Cavan, and left the paternal wing in Ireland at the age of seventeen, locating in London. His son, Henry William Washington, born in London, father of George of Melbourne, settled in the Isle of Man about 1866, and became manager of the Manx Northern Railway. He married Miss Emily Isabella Kelly, of Ballaqueeny, Isle of Man, and subsequently emigrated to Australia, dying in 1891. Mrs. Washington, née Kelly, is still living. The children are:

1. Herbert Henry Washington, born June 4, 1869, in the Isle of Man ; now in the service of the National Bank of Australia (Melbourne).

2. Walter Tom, born July 17, 1870, at Douglas, Isle of Man, is connected with the Union Bank of Australia; married Miss Alice Gillett, of Melbourne.

3. George William, born Feb. 19, 1874, at Douglas, Isle of Man, is in the service of the Union Bank of Australia.

4. John Lawrence, born June 27, 1882, at Douglas, Isle of Man; like the others, a resident of Melbourne.

5. Amy Isabel, born Jan. 1, 1877, at Douglas, Isle of Man, has been awarded the diploma of the Musical Society of Victoria for piano and harmony.

6. Florence Elizabeth, born June 16, 1878, is studying voice production under Signor Buzzi, the first Italian master of Australia.

* * * * * * * *

The letter in my possession from Mr. Joseph Washington, Bryansford, Ireland, also deserves special mention. In it the writer says : " My father, James Washington, came so young to this place that he could tell but little of his people. He had six children, three boys and three girls. Of these children, all have passed away except myself. With my family, I live on a farm on the estate of the Earl of Roden, within some three miles of a pleasant watering place, much frequented in summer. Some seasons ago, among the strangers visiting there was a family of Washingtons. Our religion is Roman Catholic. My eldest brother bore the name James, and my eldest sister was named Sarah. I have a son James Washington, so you see the family name is perpetuated."

Mr. Dudley Washington, writing from Kilgarrow, County Roscommon, says : " There are probably over forty members of our family in America at present. My father, four brothers, two sisters, two sons and a daughter, are there, and each of them has a family. I have ten cousins

in America, each having a family. One of these cousins is named George Washington and he has several children. Years ago, before emigration took such a head, I have seen over one hundred of the name in this parish of Kilglass."

* * * * * * * *

It cannot be stated when the first Irish Washington came to the United States. Neither can it be said what part of Ireland he arrived from, nor where he settled on his arrival here. That many of the name have come at different periods to the great republic of the West has already been shown, however. Mr. Michael Washington, of Providence, R. I., already mentioned, is the earliest of whom the writer has trace. He immigrated from County Galway some fifty or sixty years ago, locating, as has been stated, in Providence. After he had sufficiently arranged matters, he sent to Ireland for his wife, Catherine (Ford), and three of the children. Two children remained in the old country, but came over later. They were Patrick and Bridget. Michael Washington, the father, was a sturdy, industrious man, of that magnificent Irish type which has done so much to build, defend, and perpetuate the republic. He found on his arrival in Providence large numbers of his countrymen, — strong-limbed, stout-hearted, whole-souled ; men who were ardently patriotic, true to the New Land, but not forgetting the Old. The children of Michael and Catherine (Ford) Washington were :

(1) Ned, who is deceased. (2) Bridget, who married Thomas Norton ; she is a widow, residing in Providence. (3) Julia, who married Roderick Hunt ; she also is a widow, living in Providence. (4) Patrick, who lives in Providence. (5) Michael, who wedded Mary Sherry ; she is dead ; he resides in Providence. Three sons of Michael and Mary (Sherry) Washington are living, one

of them in Fall River, Mass., and the two others in Providence, R. I.

Patrick Washington, son of Michael, the immigrant, was one of the children who remained in Ireland, but subsequently came out. He wedded Bridget Sullivan in Providence, R. I., over thirty years ago, the ceremony being performed in that city by Rev. Father Kelly, of St. Joseph's Catholic Church. The family resides at 293 Pearl Street, Providence. The children are: (1) Edward Henry, a jeweler by trade, but now a member of the Providence Fire Department. (2) Frank, who is a piano tuner. (3) Joseph, in the provision business. (4) George Augustine, a music teacher. (5) Mary, who is at home.

* * * * * * * *

There is another Washington family in Providence, R. I., of Irish origin. It is represented by Joseph, a son of John and Mary Washington. John and Mary were of County Galway, their children being: (1) Bridget, who wedded Michael Whalen and still lives in Galway. (2) Mary, who is dead, married Michael Feeney, Central Falls, R. I., the ceremony being performed by Rev. Father Halligan, of St. Mary's Catholic Church, Pawtucket, R. I. ; had three children : Mary Jane, George Arthur, and Katie. (3) Ellen, dead ; (4) Kate, dead ; (5) Joseph (above mentioned) ; (6) John, in Australia; (7) Edward.

Of the foregoing children, Joseph (5) wedded Margaret Myer, of Lawrence, Mass. She was born in England, of Irish parents. The children are: (1) Edward ; (2) Christopher ; (3) William Joseph, deceased.

William Washington, related to this second Providence family, married twice, and was lately residing in McKeesport, Penn. He was a soldier in the American Civil War. The children are: (1) John ; (2) Joseph ; (3) Lizzie ; (4) Gertie.

30

James Washington, a brother of William, is dead. He also resided in McKeesport. His children were: (1) John ; (2) Edward ; (3) Frank ; (4) Raymond.

Michael Washington, a brother of William and James, resided in the State of Ohio, but is dead. Another brother, Patrick, served in the Civil War.

Kate Washington, likewise of this family, married a Connolley, or Conley, in Providence, R. I. She is dead.

Another Irish Washington has been heard of in Bangor, Maine. His name was Thomas ; he died in Bangor a few years ago. He is mentioned as having been a member of the Ancient Order of Hibernians, and is thought to have been from Galway.

A Julia Washington, Irish, is heard from in Lowell or Lawrence, Mass. She married there, but her husband's name I do not now recall.

* * * * * * * *

Mr. George Washington, of Dublin, co-author with me of the present little work, was born in Rathmines, Dublin, Nov. 2, 1860. When a few months old his family moved to Waterford where his father had received an appointment under the board of education. There George grew up. In 1877 his father died. George went through the Training College in Dublin with the intention of becoming a teacher. He taught a large school in County Galway for a year, but it being uncongenial work he relinquished it and embarked in business in Dublin. After spending nine years at the tea and wine trade with a leading house there, he was induced to accept a position with the largest wholesale tea and wine firm in Ireland (a Dublin house), and remained with it about five years. His ability as a man of business being widely recognized, he was next offered, and accepted, a position with the Phœnix porter brewery of Dublin, which he has represented for several

GEORGE WASHINGTON, BELFAST, IRELAND.
Died 1871, aged 47 years; was an ardent Nationalist and is believed to have been connected with the Fenian organization.

years. Of the immediate family of Irish Washingtons to which this George belongs there remain now but his sisters, Mary and Jane, his brother James' widow, and her child, "Jim," and himself. Mr. Washington, who is unmarried, is a highly educated gentleman and takes great interest in genealogical pursuits.

THE AMERICAN PRESIDENT.

LETTERS OF GEN. GEORGE WASHINGTON TO IRISH ORGANI-
ZATIONS. — HE AUTHORIZES THE COUNTERSIGN "ST.
PATRICK" ON THE SURRENDER OF BOSTON BY
THE BRITISH.

BY THOMAS HAMILTON MURRAY.

It is not my purpose at present to investigate the claim
sometimes put forth, that Mary Ball, Gen. Washington's
mother, was of Irish descent. I have seen a statement to
the effect that she was of the Balls of Dublin, members of
which family may have emigrated to England. Neither
shall I now take up the conjecture that John Washington,
the immigrant ancestor of the American president, spent
some years in Ireland, and married there, before coming
to America. These are matters for special treatment at
some future time. The ancestry of Jane Butler, mother
of Lawrence Washington, who was half brother to Gen.
George, may also be included under this head, as a subject
for future investigation.

I merely wish to show at this time the cordial relations
that existed between General Washington and those of
his countrymen who were of Irish blood. It is an established fact, which no amount of sophistry can shake, that
a very large part of the rank and file of the patriot army
of the Revolution was of Irish birth or descent. Several
of the more prominent generals were of this blood, while
the number of regimental commanders, minor officers and
privates ran well up into the thousands. The Irish ele-

ment was also handsomely represented in the navy of the young republic. At one time during the war, twenty-seven members of the Friendly Sons of St. Patrick, Phil-adelphia, subscribed £103,500 in aid of the patriot cause.

*   *   *   *   *   *   *   *

Upon the evacuation of Boston by the British, March 17, 1776, the Americans marched in and took possession. The siege had lasted several months. The countersign authorized by Washington for that day of triumph was "St. Patrick," and the brigadier of the day was Gen. John Sullivan. At a meeting in Philadelphia, Dec. 17, 1781, of the Friendly Sons of St. Patrick, already men tioned, Washington was made an "adopted Irishman," so to speak, by being admitted to membership. A few days later, upon being presented with an address, and the insignia or medal of the organization, he made the following reply : —

SIR :

I accept with singular pleasure, the Ensign of so worthy a Fraternity as that of the Sons of St. Patrick in this city. — a Society distinguished for the firm Adherence of its Members to the glorious cause in which we are embarked.

Give me leave to assure you, Sir, that I shall never cast my eyes upon the badge with which I am Honoured, but with a grateful remembrance of the polite and affectionate manner in which it was presented.

I am, with Respect and Esteem, Sir,
Your mo. ob. Servant,
GEORGE WASHINGTON.

To GEORGE CAMPBELL, Esq., President of the Society of the Friendly Sons of St. Patrick, in the city of Philadelphia.

*   *   *   *   *   *   *   *

Washington dined with the Friendly Sons on at least three occasions, viz.: Jan. 1, 1782, March 18, 1782, and June 18, 1787. A party of Irish gentlemen, most of them

belonging to the Irish Volunteers, arrived in New York
from Ireland in November, 1783, and addressed congratu-
lations to Washington on the successful termination of the
American Revolution. To this address Washington thus
replied: —

*To the Members of the Volunteer Association and other
inhabitants of the Kingdom of Ireland who have lately
arrived in the city of New York : —*

GENTLEMEN : The testimony of your satisfaction at
the glorious termination of the late contest, and your in-
dulgent opinion of my agency in it, afford me singular
pleasure and merit my warmest acknowledgment. If the
example of the Americans, successfully contended in the
cause of freedom, can be of any use to other nations, we
shall have an additional motive for rejoicing at so prosperous an event.

It was not an uninteresting consideration to learn that
the Kingdom of Ireland, by a bold and manly conduct, had
obtained the redress of many of its grievances ; and it is
much to be wished that the blessings of equal liberty and
unrestrained commerce may yet prevail more extensively.
In the meantime, you may be assured, gentlemen, that the
hospitality and beneficence of your countrymen to our
brethren, who have been prisoners of war, are neither unknown nor unregarded.

The bosom of America is open to receive not only the
opulent and respectable stranger, but the oppressed and
persecuted of all nations and religions, whom we shall
welcome to a participation in all our rights and privileges,
if by decency and propriety of conduct they appear to
merit the enjoyment.

GEORGE WASHINGTON.

*   *   *   *   *   *   *   *

Various organizations in Ireland also sent congratula-
tions. One of these bodies was the Yankee Club, of
Stewartstown, Tyrone. Washington, replying to its good

35

1593362

wishes, Jan. 20, 1784, and writing from Mount Vernon, said : —

GENTLEMEN : It is with unfeigned satisfaction that I accept your congratulation on the late happy and glorious revolution. . . . If, in the course of our successful contest, good consequences have resulted to the oppressed Kingdom of Ireland, it will afford a new source of felicitation to all who respect the interests of humanity.

＊　＊　＊　＊　＊　＊　＊　＊

General Washington's esteem for the people of Ireland and for the Irish in his command is further illustrated by the order issued by him for the observance of St. Patrick's day, 1780.

In the St. Louis *Republican*, October, 1887, appears the following : —

Quite an interesting and curious old manuscript relating to the time of the American Revolution has been discovered by one of our reporters. It is in the possession of a resident of St. Louis. It is no less then the original " military orders of the day " issued to the " Main Guard and Morristown Picket " from February 15 to April 7, 1780, while the American army, under Gen. Washington, was stationed at Morristown, N. J.

Though musty with age, and on that account in some places almost illegible, the manuscript as a whole is as clear as on the days it was written, and presents a photograph of the interior workings of that famous little American army, its morale, its soldierly discipline, the character of the common soldiers, the manner in which they were provided for, the kind of arms with which they were equipped, and of other incidents, as even the very pastimes and amusements allowed the soldiers — such as perhaps no historian of that period has ever presented to the world. At present only two extracts from the manuscript are given, and they are selected for the purpose of showing how this nation, in the throes of its birth, as heartily as it does now in the plenitude of its might and power, sympathized with the Irish people : —

36

"HEADQUARTERS, March 16, 1780.

Officers for duty to-morrow : Brig-Gen. Clinton, Maj. Edwards, Brig.-Maj. Brice. The General [Washington] congratulates the army on the very interesting proceedings of the parliament of Ireland and of the inhabitants of the country, which have been lately communicated. Not only do they appear calculated to remove the heavy and tyrannical oppressions on their trade, but to restore to a brave and generous people their ancient rights and privileges, and in their operation to promote the cause of America. Desirous of impressing on the mind of the army transactions so important in their nature, the General directs that all fatigue and working parties cease for to-morrow, the 17th, [a] day held in particular regard by the people of that nation. At the same time that he orders this as a mark of pleasure he feels in the situation, he persuades himself that the celebration of the day will not be attended by the least rioting or disorder. The officers to be at their quarters in camp, and the troops of each State are to be in their own encampment.

Division orders : Captain of the day to-morrow, brigadier-major from the Second Pennsylvania brigade.

Brigade orders : Captain of the day [name illegible]. Adjutant of the day to-morrow, Herbert —— ."

Following is another extract : —

" DIVISION ORDERS, March 17, 1780. — The commanding officer desires that the celebration of the day should not pass by without having a little rum issued to the troops, and has thought proper to direct the commissary to send for the hogshead which the colonel has purchased already in the vicinity of the camp. While the troops are celebrating the bravery of St. Patrick in innocent mirth and pastime, he hopes they will not forget their worthy friends in the kingdom of Ireland, who, with the greatest unanimity, have stepped forward in opposition to the tyrant Great Britain, and who, like us, are determined to die or be free. The troops will conduct themselves with the greatest sobriety and good order."

MISS EVELYN MACNAMARA,
Daughter of Nicholas J. MacNamara, Galway, Ireland,
and of Margaret Washington, his wife.

37

The manuscript, continues the *Republican*, from which the above extracts are taken, bears internal evidence of its genuineness, and is, besides, vouched for by a St. Louis lady, who holds it a precious heirloom from her grandfather, an officer of the Revolutionary war, in the " Main Guard and Morristown Picket."

Gaine's New York *Mercury*, April 24, 1780, also contains the foregoing congratulatory order of Washington, its version agreeing in all essential respects with that produced in the St. Louis *Republican*, and differing only in some minor points of phraseology.

SOME BIRTHS OF WASHINGTONS IN IRELAND DURING AND SINCE 1864.

COMPILED FROM OFFICIAL SOURCES.

Margaret Washington, Waterford, 1864.
Patrick Washington, New Ross (Wexford), 1865.
Catherine Washington, Gort (Galway), 1866.
Jane Alice Washington, Waterford.
Margaret Washington, Gort.
John Washington, Gort, 1869.
Bridget'Washington, New Ross, 1869.
Thomas Washington, Waterford.
Thomas Joseph Washington, Thurles (Tipperary), 1869.
James Joseph Washington, Kilkeel (County Down), 1870.
John Joseph Washington, Waterford.
Martin Washington, Gort.
Edmund Denis Washington, Dublin, 1871.
James Joseph Washington, Boyle, 1871.
James Washington, Thurles, 1871.
George Washington, Belfast, 1871.
Peter Washington, New Ross, 1872.
Patrick Washington, Enniskillen (Fermanagh), 1873.
Elizabeth Washington, New Ross, 1875.
Mary Washington, New Ross, 1875.
Francis Washington, Strokestown (Rosconimon), 1877.
Catherine Washington, New Ross, 1878.
Samuel Patrick Washington, Dublin, 1878.
Elizabeth'Washington, New Ross, 1880.
Thomas Washington, Strokestown, 1881.

39

Margaret Washington, New Ross, 1882.
Thomas Washington, New Ross, 1883.
Edmund Washington, Strokestown.
Thomas Washington, New Ross, 1885.
Wilhelmina Washington, Belfast.
Ellen Washington, Strokestown.
Peter Washington, New Ross.
Patrick Washington, Strokestown, 1886.
Dudley Washington, Strokestown.
Thos. Alexander Washington, Limerick.
Ann Kate Washington, Strokestown, 1890.
Elizabeth Washington, New Ross.

DEATHS OF IRISH WASHINGTONS DURING AND SINCE 1864.

COMPILED FROM OFFICIAL SOURCES.

Ellen Washington, Cork, 1864.
Mary Washington, Thomastown, 1864.
James Washington, Strokestown, 1866.
Thomas Washington, Gort.
Mary Washington, Strokestown, 1869.
Elizabeth Washington, Strokestown, 1869.
John Washington, Gort, 1869.
Thomas J. Washington, Thurles, 1870.
John Washington, Carlow, 1870.
John Joseph Washington, Waterford, 1870.
George Washington, Belfast, 1871.
John Washington, New Ross. 1871.

40

Judy Washington, Thurles, 1872.
Sarah Washington, Kilkeel, 1874.
Thomas Washington, Kilkenny, 1874.
James Washington, Kilkeel, 1875.
Mary Washington, Callan (County Kilkenny), 1875.
James Washington, Waterford, 1877.
Thomas Washington, Strokestown, 1878.
John Washington, Strokestown, 1880.
Kate Washington, Coroffin (County Clare), 1886.
Lizzie Washington, Strokestown, 1890.

SOME OTHER
MENTION OF IRISH WASHINGTONS.

EXTRACTS FROM MARRIAGE LICENSE BONDS (PROTESTANT).

Diocese of Meath, 1842, Sarah Washington and Andrew McKey.

Diocese of Ossory, 1762, Mary Washington and Alexander Ward.

Diocese of Armagh, 1829, Elizabeth Washington, otherwise Stewart, and Richard Dowse.

IRISH WASHINGTONS OR THEIR DESCEND-
ANTS IN PROVIDENCE, RHODE ISLAND,
(LIVING OR DEAD).

Michael Washington, first of the name.
Catherine (Ford) Washington, his wife.
Edward Washington, dead.
Patrick Washington, 293 Pearl Street.
Michael Washington.
Edward Henry Washington, fire department.
Frank Washington, piano tuner.
Joseph Washington, provision business.
George Augustine Washington, music teacher.
Mary Washington.
Howard Washington.
Ellen Washington, dead.
Kate Washington, dead.
Joseph Washington.
Edward Washington.
Edward Washington (2).
Christopher Washington.
William Joseph Washington, dead.
Bridget Washington, married Thomas Norton.
Julia Washington, married Roderick Hunt.
Mary Washington, married Michael Feeney, Pawtucket or
    Central Falls, R. I.
John Washington (now believed to be in Australia).

IRISH WASHINGTONS IN PENNSYLVANIA.

William Washington, McKeesport.
John Washington, McKeesport.
Joseph Washington, McKeesport.
Lizzie Washington, McKeesport.
Gertie Washington, McKeesport.
James Washington, McKeesport.
John Washington (2), McKeesport.
Edward Washington, McKeesport.
Frank Washington, McKeesport.
Raymond Washington, McKeesport.
Michael Washington, resided in Ohio; dead.
Patrick Washington, soldier in American Civil War; whereabouts unknown.

WASHINGTONS IN ENGLAND, OF PATERNAL IRISH DESCENT.

(THE MANCHESTER BRANCH.)

George Washington, married Alice Doyxe.
George Washington, married Mary Raby.
Alice Washington, married William Baguley.
Henry Washington, dead.
Gertrude Washington.
Ethel Washington.
Alice Washington.
George Washington, dead.
Harry Washington.
Martha Washington, dead.
Mary Washington, dead.

WASHINGTONS OF IRISH DESCENT IN AUSTRALIA.

Henry William Washington, died 1891.
Herbert Henry Washington, Melbourne.
Walter Tom Washington, Melbourne.
George William Washington, Melbourne.
John Lawrence Washington, Melbourne.
Amy Isabel Washington, Melbourne.
Florence Elizabeth Washington, Melbourne.
John Washington (of the Rhode Island family).